WILL ROGERS

COWBOY, COMEDIAN, AND COMMENTATOR

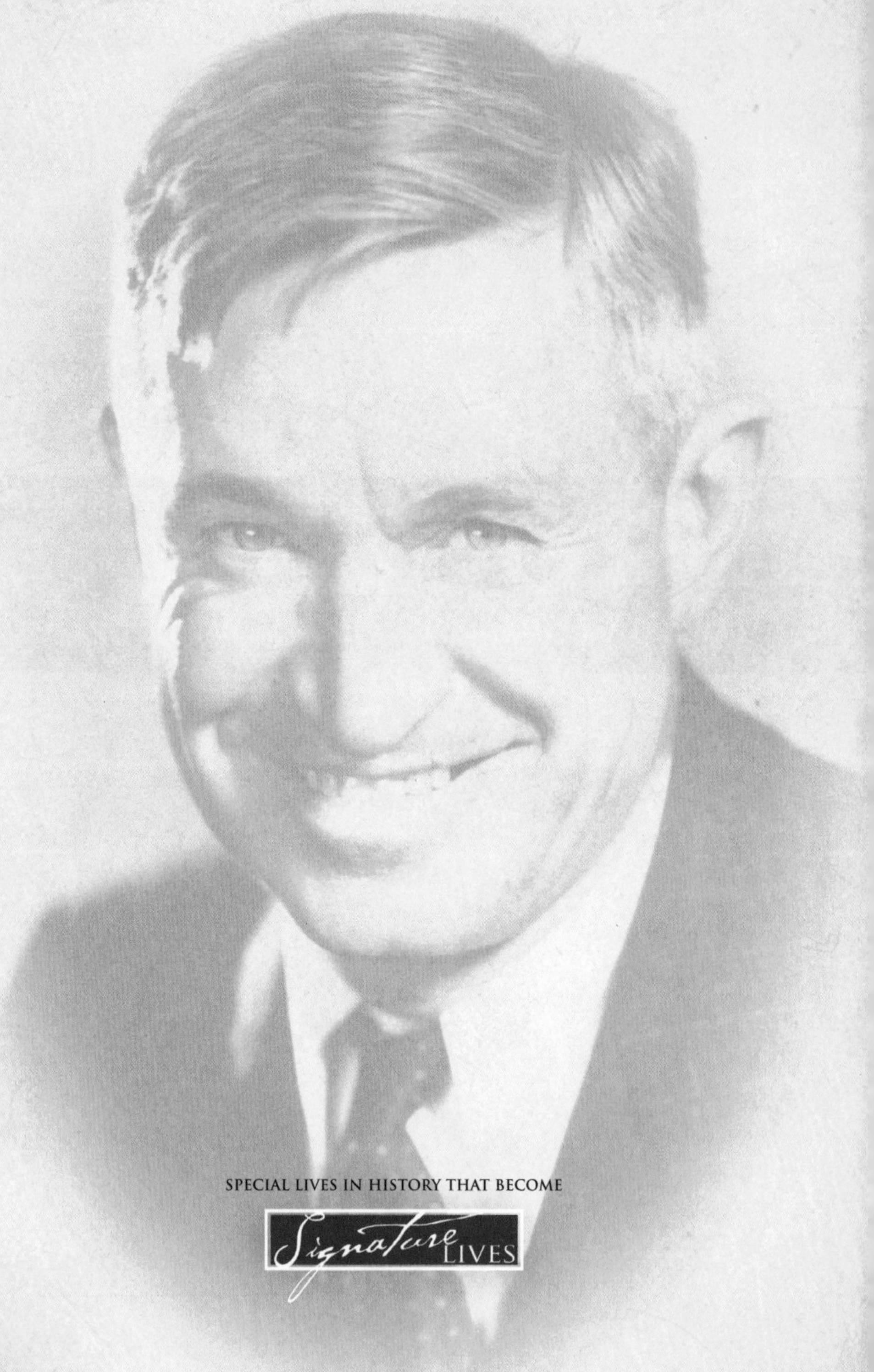

SPECIAL LIVES IN HISTORY THAT BECOME

Signature LIVES

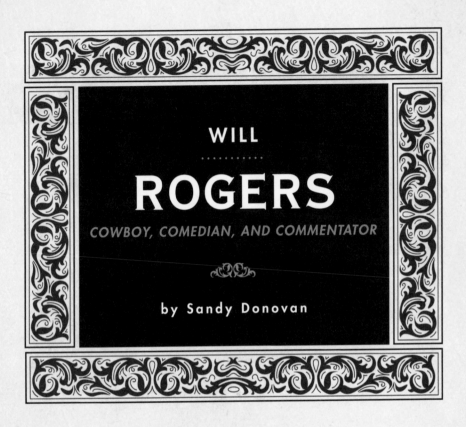

WILL

ROGERS

COWBOY, COMEDIAN, AND COMMENTATOR

by Sandy Donovan

Content Adviser: Steven K. Gragert,
Interim Director,
Will Rogers Memorial Museum

Reading Adviser: Rosemary G. Palmer, Ph.D.,
Department of Literacy, College of Education,
Boise State University

Compass Point Books ◈ Minneapolis, Minnesota

Compass Point Books
3109 West 50th Street, #115
Minneapolis, MN 55410

Visit Compass Point Books on the Internet at *www.compasspointbooks.com*
or e-mail your request to *custserv@compasspointbooks.com*

Editor: Anthony Wacholtz
Page Production: Noumenon Creative
Photo Researcher: Svetlana Zhurkin
Cartographer: XNR Productions, Inc.
Library Consultant: Kathleen Baxter

Art Director: Jaime Martens
Creative Director: Keith Griffin
Editorial Director: Carol Jones
Managing Editor: Catherine Neitge

Library of Congress Cataloging-in-Publication Data
Donovan, Sandra, 1967–
   Will Rogers: cowboy, comedian, and commentator / by Sandy Donovan.
      p. cm.—(Signature lives)
   Includes bibliographical references and index.
   ISBN-13: 978-0-7565-2463-0 (library binding)
   ISBN-10: 0-7565-2463-6 (library binding)
   ISBN-13: 978-0-7565-3205-5 (paperback)
   ISBN-10: 0-7565-3205-1 (paperback)
   1. Rogers, Will, 1879-1935—Juvenile literature. 2. Entertainers—United
States—Biography—Juvenile literature. 3. Humorists, American—20th
century—Biography—Juvenile literature. I. Title. II. Series.
   PN2287.R74D66 2006
   792.702'8092—dc22   2006027077

Signature Lives

MODERN AMERICA

Starting in the late 19th century, advancements in all areas of human activity transformed an old world into a new and modern place. Inventions prompted rapid shifts in lifestyle, and scientific discoveries began to alter the way humanity viewed itself. Beginning with World War I, warfare took place on a global scale, and ideas such as nationalism and communism showed that countries were taking a larger view of their place in the world. The combination of all these changes continues to produce what we know as the modern world.

Table of Contents

1 FROM OKLAHOMA TO BEVERLY HILLS

ｃ✄✄Ｄ

The California sky was filled with rain clouds, and a downpour drenched the crowd gathered outside the swanky Beverly Hills Hotel. But the weather was not dampening the enthusiasm of the day. Between the umbrellas were large, draping banners and handheld signs that read, "Beverly Hills Welcomes Mayor Will Rogers" and "We Love Our Mayor Will."

Beverly Hills, home to most of Hollywood's greatest stars, had declared Will Rogers its honorary mayor. The "mayor," his wife, Betty, and their three children soon arrived in a Rolls Royce. They had been led by motorcade from the Los Angeles train station upon their return from a national tour of sold-out speaking engagements by Will Rogers. The crowd erupted as the 47-year-old star of stage, screen, and

Will Rogers was a Hollywood star in the early 1900s.

print emerged to address the audience.

The scene at the hotel on December 22, 1926, was in stark contrast to Will Rogers' boyhood in Indian Territory, now the state of Oklahoma, where he was first introduced to the art of roping. But that was just what the public loved most about Rogers. He could move easily between the ranch houses of his cowboy youth and the celebrity-packed theaters of New York and Hollywood.

Rogers gave a speech to a jubilant crowd after becoming the honorary mayor of Beverly Hills.

To millions of adoring fans across the country, he spoke and wrote with folksy elegance about America's families, government, and way of life. Throughout the 1920s and early 1930s, as America went through the Roaring Twenties and the Great Depression, Rogers told Americans what they needed to hear to feel safe and understood.

Will Rogers would become America's most popular movie star, newspaper columnist, and radio personality. Throughout his career, his popularity stemmed from his ability to connect with people from all walks of life. It was reflected in his most famous quotation: "I never met a man I didn't like."

His ongoing sense of adventure, which led him to small towns across America and remote spots around the globe, contrasted with the simple wisdom that his words communicated. He reminded people that life should never be more complicated than the cowboy setting of his youth in Oklahoma. ❧

Chapter

2 WILD WEST BOYHOOD

❦

Will Rogers was born into adventure. His grandfather, Robert Rogers Jr., was one of the first Cherokee Indians to move from the southeastern part of the country to Indian Territory in the west, which later became the state of Oklahoma. The Rogers family and other Cherokee Indians built the thriving society known as the Cherokee Nation on the rich farmlands of Indian Territory. The lush, wide-open land was suited to raising cattle, and cattle ranching became their way of life.

Robert's son, Clement Vann Rogers, became a political leader and wealthy rancher, with about 60,000 acres (24,000 hectares) of cattle-grazing land along the Verdigris River in northeastern Oklahoma. Clem married a young part-Cherokee woman, Mary

Clem Rogers (standing, far left) was part of a Cherokee committee that met with representatives from the U.S. government to discuss the allotment of land to Indians.

In the late 1800s, most
Indian Territory inhab-
itants were Cherokee
Indians forced to move
from Georgia, North
and South Carolina,
Alabama, and
Tennessee. Some went
west in the 1820s and
early 1830s, but most
were removed from
their southeastern
homes in 1838 and
escorted west by the
U.S. Army. During
this difficult march,
known as the Trail of
Tears, an estimated
4,000 Cherokee died.
The ones who arrived
in Indian Territory
sought to rebuild
their Cherokee Nation.
They brought along
a taste for Southern
food, architecture,
and other Southern
practices, including
slavery. Most wealthy
Cherokee Nation
leaders, including
Clem Rogers, owned
slaves.

Schrimsher, shortly before the Civil War reached Indian Territory. During the Civil War, Clem fought for the Confederates and lost almost all of his estate. Union soldiers plundered his farm, destroyed his house, and set his cattle free. But by the 1880s, Clem had rebuilt his ranch and was elected to the Cherokee Nation senate.

Clem and Mary's first daughter, Elizabeth, was born in 1861, before Clem went to war. When fighting approached the ranch, Mary took the baby and headed south to stay with relatives, but the baby died during the journey. Another daughter, Sallie, was born in 1863, and a son, Robert, followed in 1866. A daughter, Maud, was born in 1869. During the 1870s, the Rogers had three more children, but only one of them, Mary, lived past infancy. By the time William Penn Adair Rogers was born, his parents were both 40 years old, and three of his four siblings were teenagers. Willie, as his family called him, was born

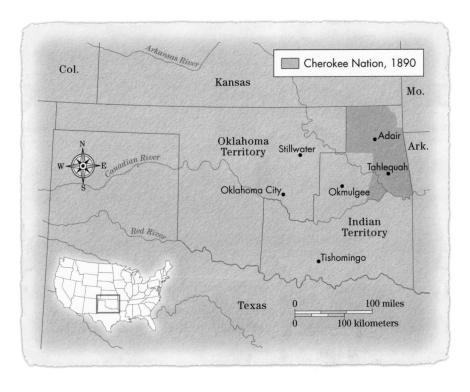

Col.

Arkansas River

Kansas

Mo.

Cherokee Nation, 1890

Oklahoma
Territory

Stillwater

Adair

Ark.

N
W—E
S

Canadian River

Tahlequah

Oklahoma City

Okmulgee

Red River

Indian
Territory

Tishomingo

Texas

0   100 miles

0   100 kilometers

on November 4, 1879, in the Rogers' two-story, seven-room house overlooking the Verdigris River near present-day Oolagah, Oklahoma.

Clem and Mary, like many Cherokee Indians of the 19th century, were of mixed blood. They were each about one-fourth Cherokee. This made their children about one-fourth Cherokee as well—the rest of their ancestry was Scottish, Irish, and either Dutch or German. Although the couple had similar Cherokee backgrounds, Clem and Mary possessed opposite personalities. Clem was silent and stern with a reputation as a serious, fair businessman.

By 1890, the Cherokee Nation occupied a small region in north-eastern Indian Territory.

With blue eyes and blond hair, he looked Scottish and Irish, but not Cherokee. Mary, on the other hand, was sweet, talkative, and humorous, and she loved music. She had the straight black hair and narrow cheekbones of her Cherokee ancestors. Willie's parents had other differences as well. Mary was a devout Methodist, but Clem was not religious. Also, Mary had graduated from high school, but Clem had dropped out of school.

Mary Rogers instilled a love of talk, stories, and music in her children.

Despite these differences, the Rogers had a happy and successful marriage. While Clem oversaw the ranch, Mary managed the household and children. Many people said that Will Rogers got his cowboy skills from his father and his sense of humor from his mother. Once, a visiting cowboy was silently admiring one of Mary's babies. Mary broke the silence by saying:

> *I know exactly what you're thinking. You're thinking this is the homeliest baby you ever saw.*

*Will Rogers'
childhood home*

Another time, she baked and served a cotton-stuffed pie to a cowboy who often played jokes on her.

Thanks to Mary, the Rogers' house became the social center of the area. Daylong parties featuring large meals, music, and dancing were common. The house looked like a Southern plantation, with sculptured flower beds, arching trees, a white picket fence, and white columns supporting upstairs and downstairs porches along the front. Inside, it was elegantly decorated with a grand piano, lace curtains, and upholstered furniture.

Although Willie grew up in this elegant house, his childhood was essentially a Wild West cowboy experience. As a toddler, he watched his father and older brother, Robert, leave early each morning to work on the ranch, rounding up cattle for counting

Will grew up on a ranch among cowboys riding horses and roping cattle.

and branching. While they were gone, Willie spent half of each day pretending to be a cowboy and the other half listening to his mother's stories and songs.

The world changed for Willie when he was 3. In the spring of 1883, his brother Robert, who was almost 17, died unexpectedly of pneumonia. Now Willie was the only son, and he began to act the part of rancher and cowboy more and more. He learned to ride a horse by the time he was 4 and spent most of the day trotting across the ranch on his horse. When he was 5, his father bought him his own cream-colored pony named Comanche. Willie and Comanche were soon inseparable. A cousin even described them as being "almost like Siamese twins." Will spent hours on Comanche, perfecting the skills that would eventually make him well-known.

Although Will Rogers did not always emphasize his roots as a Cherokee Indian, he remained proud of being part Cherokee. He once said, "I have Indian Blood in me. I have just enough white blood for you to question my honesty!"

3 LEARNING THE ROPES

❦

Two skills are essential to a cowboy: riding horses and "roping," or throwing lariats. While Willie demonstrated his riding abilities from an early age, he was more interested in roping. Before he could talk or walk, he watched his father and other ranch workers throwing lariats, not only to rope cattle, but also to have fun. By the time he was 5, Willie was spending countless hours watching Dan Walker—a worker on the Rogers' ranch and an excellent roper—throw his lariat. Willie practiced throwing his own lariat around a tree stump in his backyard for hours each day.

Willie had to cut back on his roping time when he began attending school at age 7. The school was 12 miles (19.2 kilometers) from home, so during the

Will Rogers (left) with his childhood friend and schoolmate, Charley McClellan

Sallie Rogers allowed Will to stay with her after he started going to school.

week, he lived with his older married sister, Sallie, who lived 3 miles (4.8 km) from the school. Willie made the daily trip to the schoolhouse on horseback. His father gave him a special saddle with his initials, WPR, stamped on the back. Like his father, though, Willie had little interest in school. His sister later recalled that she watched him closely as he rode away to make sure he was headed toward the school.

By age 10, Willie's roping skills were amazing. He practiced whenever he had the chance—at school, his sister's house, or his own house on weekends. After one year at school, Willie's father transferred him to Harrell Institute, a Methodist boarding school in the town of Muskogee, Oklahoma. Although Harrell was a school for girls, Willie was accepted because he was the same age as the superintendent's son and could share a room with him. He found his new school to be as good a place as any to perfect his roping tricks.

But in May 1890, Willie's happy childhood came to an abrupt end when his mother died unexpectedly of a stomach virus. For most of his life, Will Rogers did not talk about how difficult it was to lose his mother at such an early age. His wife later said that he never really got over it. "He cried when he told me about it many years later," she said. "It left in him a lonely, lost feeling that persisted long after he was successful and famous." His father tried to soften the blow by giving Willie 75 calves of his very own. Willie was an official cowboy now, with his own small herd to care for.

In the fall of 1892, Willie enrolled at another new school, Willie Halsell College. The school was in the railroad town of Vinita, about 40 miles (64 km) northeast of the Rogers ranch. As far as Will was concerned, the biggest impact was that the school year was longer than at his old school. With classes scheduled until the middle of June, Willie wrote to his best friend, "We will miss all the roundups, won't we?"

The word lariat comes from the Spanish phrase la riata, meaning "the rope." Made from strips of rawhide, horsehair, or hemp braided together, lariats were used to rein in cattle. If one cow escaped the herd, a cowboy on horseback could quickly rope it and bring it back. Lariats were usually 40 to 50 feet (12.2 to 15.3 meters) long and were carried coiled up in a loop. A few simple throws were all a cowboy needed to know. But perfecting specialty throws became an art form practiced by cowboys throughout the American West in the late 19th and early 20th centuries.

By his second year at Halsell, Willie was beginning to enjoy the school. His classmates nicknamed him "Rabbit" because he was fast and had big ears. Although his grades weren't great—he only made the honor roll twice—he found one subject that he enjoyed: elocution, or public speaking. The local newspaper wrote, "Willie Rogers ... never failed to receive a hearty round of applause." He came in second in the schoolwide elocution contest, receiving a duplicate gold medal for his performance.

By the end of his first year at Halsell, he had dropped the nickname Willie. As he developed his speaking skills, he continued his obsession with roping. In the summer of 1893, Will took a trip with his father to the World's Columbian Exposition in Chicago. There he saw Buffalo Bill's Wild West show featuring the great Mexican cowboy Vincente Oropeza. He was a wizard with a lariat and dazzled Will and others in the crowd with specialty tricks. Oropeza performed intricate dances with his lariat, twirling it vertically and horizontally, making figure eights and other shapes, and jumping in and out of the loops.

Will returned to school with renewed excitement about roping and began to rope anything that moved. Students on campus began dragging their feet everywhere they walked in order to avoid being roped by Will.

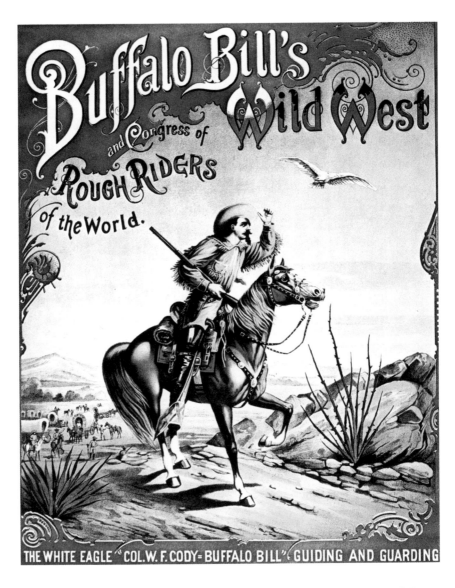

THE WHITE EAGLE "COL. W. F. CODY=BUFFALO BILL" GUIDING AND GUARDING

After four years at Halsell, Will transferred to Scarritt College in Missouri. Despite its name, Scarritt College was a high school. Will spent one and a half years there and impressed people with his practical

Buffalo Bill Cody and his Rough Riders put on a spectacular show at the World's Columbian Exposition.

Will (seated, third from left) joined the football team at Scarritt College.

jokes. He once roped a teacher's horse, which ruined a picket fence and a tennis court backdrop. Years later, one of his Scarritt teachers said that nobody could have "predicted that the funny fellow we knew as Will Rogers would be anything but mediocre or live anything but an absurdly uneventful life."

Probably because Will did so poorly in his classes and continued to get in trouble for his practical jokes, his father sent him to Kemper School, a Missouri military school, in the winter of 1897. This was the last of six schools he attended. He liked Kemper even less than his other schools. He earned only average grades, struggling most with algebra and physics, and he continued to get into trouble. At the military school, students earned demerits, or points, whenever they got in trouble. For each demerit, students had to spend one hour doing chores around the school. Will earned plenty of demerits for playing practical jokes with his lariat, and he earned more for hiding his lariat under his shirt so teachers couldn't confiscate it.

By February 1898, Will had earned 150 demerits. He had also turned 18, and he was tired of school. He wanted to experience life as a real cowboy. So when he heard from a classmate that jobs were available at a ranch in Texas, Will wrote to two of his sisters, asking for money. The night the money arrived, he left his dormitory and bought a train ticket to Texas. There he found a job at Ewing Ranch that paid $30 a month. ✍

4 CHAPTER COWBOY ADVENTURES

❦

Will loved life as a ranch hand. He was an excellent student when he was learning about things that interested him. He soon learned how to take care of huge herds of cattle and make them do what he wanted them to do. After a few months on Ewing Ranch, the owner let Will go on a cattle drive. With five other ranch hands and one cook, Will set out to move 400 cattle from the Texas ranch to a town in Kansas, 160 miles (256 km) away. The work was difficult and the traveling was slow, but Will had the time of his life. As soon as he returned, he signed up for another cattle drive with a different ranch. For six months, Will alternated between working as a ranch hand and going on cattle drives.

In the fall of 1898, school started and Will knew

it was too late for his father to make him go back. He returned to his father's ranch in Indian Territory. Clem Rogers had been angry and disappointed when Will ran away from school, but he soon realized that his son was not cut out for school. So he made him an offer: He would give Will his own herd of cattle if Will agreed to live on the ranch and manage it. Will took him up on the offer. With the help of two friends, he built himself a one-room log cabin near the ranch and settled in as a ranch manager.

Will spent almost two years managing the family ranch. As time went on, he liked it less and less. He spent too much time doing chores he found boring, such as cutting and stacking hay for the cattle to eat

Cowboys mounted on horses herded cattle on a ranch in the late 1800s.

during the winter. Also, he was used to wide-open spaces in Texas. The Rogers ranch was divided up into sections with barbed-wire fences, and when Will moved his cattle, he had to climb down from his horse to open fences. This wasn't his idea of life as a cowboy. Still, he enjoyed being back in Indian Territory, where he met old friends and made new ones.

In late 1899, Will met a 20-year-old woman from Arkansas named Betty Blake, who was visiting her sister in Indian Territory. It would take him nine years to convince Betty to marry him, but he was obviously infatuated with her from their first meeting. Shortly after she returned home to Arkansas, Will began writing her letters. In mid-March, he wrote:

> *My Dear Betty,*
> *Now for me to attempt to express my delight for your sweet letter would be utterly impossible so will just put it mildly and say I was very very much pleased. I was also surprised for I thought you had forgotten your [Cowboy] (for I am yours as far as I am concerned). ... I ought not to have got so broken up over you but I could not help it so if you do not see fit to answer this please do not say a word about it to any one for the sake of a broken hearted Cherokee Cowboy. ...*
> > *I am yours with love*
> > *Will Rogers*

Meanwhile, Will grew increasingly bored with ranch life, until he found a new interest that added excitement to his life and gave him an opportunity to travel—and even see Betty. In 1899, Will discovered "cowboy competitions," where ropers competed and showed off their lariat skills. The most thrilling of these competitions featured steer-roping contests. On July 4, 1899, he competed in a steer-roping contest near his home and won first place.

Will immediately signed up for a larger steer-roping contest at the annual fair in St. Louis. Will and his favorite horse, Comanche, traveled there by train. At the start of the contest, the relatively small Will realized he and his equally small horse would be no match for the 1,000-pound (450-kilogram) steer. Although both he and Comanche ended up on the ground, Will later wrote that the experience "gave me a touch of 'Show business' in a way." He was hooked on the showy side of cowboy life.

Despite his defeat at the St. Louis Fair, he entered more roping contests. He even managed to meet Betty Blake at a contest in

Steer roping is an American cowboy contest of skills similar to Spanish bullfighting. A cowboy waits on horseback in the middle of a fenced-in roping area with one end of a rope tied to his saddle. A steer is sent through a chute into the roping area, and a referee shouts "Go!" The cowboy then has to throw the other end of the rope around the steer's horn. Once he has roped the steer, the cowboy rides in the opposite direction to try to bring the steer to the ground.

Springfield, Missouri. During the next few years, he traveled around the southwestern United States, entering contests at state fairs, city festivals, and other events. Although he enjoyed the contests, he knew that both he and Comanche were too small to ever be top-notch roping contestants.

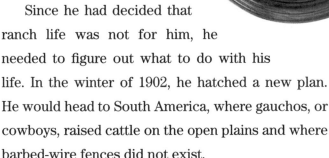

Betty Blake at age 18

Since he had decided that ranch life was not for him, he needed to figure out what to do with his life. In the winter of 1902, he hatched a new plan. He would head to South America, where gauchos, or cowboys, raised cattle on the open plains and where barbed-wire fences did not exist.

In February 1902, Will sold his herd of cattle to his father, loaned Comanche to a friend, and bought a hand-carved leather saddle. With a friend, Will set out for New Orleans, figuring he could hop on a ship to Argentina. But when they arrived in New Orleans, they found that the only ships to Argentina traveled from New York. So they took a steamer ship to New York, where they learned that the quickest way to Argentina was through England.

Will and his friend spent nine days in England before sailing to Buenos Aires, Argentina. In Argentina, they could not find jobs, it was freezing cold, and the food was nearly inedible. Will's friend headed home almost immediately. Will became broke very quickly because he loaned his friend money for the return trip. He was also homesick and lonely. After suffering through a couple of lousy jobs, he decided to try his luck in another part of the world. He got a job taking a herd of livestock on a ship bound for South Africa.

He soon found that life on the ship was even more miserable than life in Argentina. He was seasick for days on end and was assigned to be the night watchman for the cattle. He later wrote to a friend, "I will mail you a special edition of my drama '25 days on a floating dunghill.'"

Once he arrived in South Africa, Will's luck changed. He soon found work doing odd jobs. Before long, he began his official show business career when he was hired to be in Texas Jack's Wild West Show. His stage name was "The Cherokee Kid."

Will wrote home to his father, "I am getting homesick, but don't know what I would do there more than make a living. As it is, I am off here bothering and worrying no one and getting along first rate." He added in another letter to his father that he planned to come home soon, but for now "I must

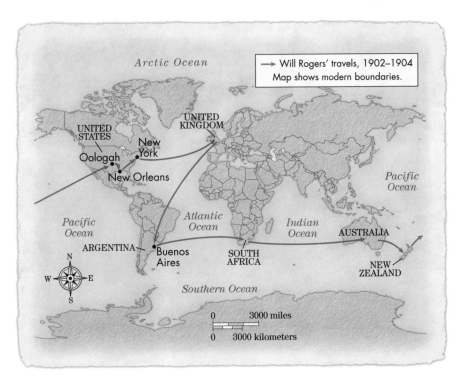

Arctic Ocean

→ Will Rogers' travels, 1902–1904
Map shows modern boundaries.

UNITED
KINGDOM

UNITED
STATES
New
York
Oologah
New Orleans

Pacific
Ocean

Atlantic
Ocean

Indian
Ocean

AUSTRALIA

Pacific
Ocean

ARGENTINA
Buenos
Aires

SOUTH
AFRICA

NEW
ZEALAND

N
W   E
S

Southern Ocean

0   3000 miles

0   3000 kilometers

Will circled the globe between 1902 and 1904 to find a lifestyle that suited him.

see a bit more." So he set off for Australia, where he joined a circus as a trick roper and toured New Zealand. Billed as "a gentleman from America with a large American accent and a splendid skill with the lasso," Will performed all of his best roping tricks in the circus. He dressed in a tight-fitting red velvet suit with gold embroidery.

When the tour ended in March 1904, Will finally set sail for home. He had been gone for two years and was eager to get back to his friends and family. ❧

Chapter

5 VAUDEVILLE CALLS

⤜⤚

By the time Rogers returned home, he had 11 nieces and nephews, so he had plenty of family to visit. He told his tales of adventures in South America, Africa, Australia, and New Zealand. But he spent less than a month in Indian Territory. As he later wrote in a letter:

> *Now I am making my own way ... and don't feel like staying at home for people would say that I was living off my Father.*

By early May 1904, Rogers set out for St. Louis. He got a job as a rider and trick roper with the Zack Mulhall Congress of Rough Riders and Ropers. This cowboy variety show was booked to perform

Zack Mulhall (front row, with his arm around his daughter Lucille) and his band of cowboys

at St. Louis' Louisiana Purchase Exposition. The Exposition marked the 100th anniversary of the United States' purchase of the Louisiana Territory from France (the celebration was actually one year late—the purchase took place in 1803). During the show, Rogers performed roping tricks and played a cowboy in "Cowboy vs. Indian" scenes. Though his name was left out of the show's program, he quickly attracted attention for his show-business personality. He had learned how to play to crowds during his time with the circus in South Africa and Australia. As one of his fellow performers remembered:

> *He had somethin' the rest of us didn't have, no matter who was around. Everybody was always lookin' at Will.*

Rogers enjoyed being in the spotlight at the fair, but he had bigger dreams. He wanted to be the star of the hottest type of entertainment at the time: vaudeville. Top vaudeville stars were famous across the country. During the 1904 exposition, he got a small job doing roping tricks at a vaudeville show at the St. Louis Standard Theater. Rogers was successful enough at this first vaudeville job that he was hired for a weeklong show in Chicago. He dazzled the audiences with his rope tricks, but he soon discovered—by accident—a way to make his

act more popular.

One night, in the middle of his act, a dog that was waiting to perform in another act ran across the stage in front of Rogers. Reacting quickly, he used his lariat to rope the dog, and the audience erupted

Vaudeville had been the most popular form of mass entertainment in America since the late 1800s. This type of theater consisted of different acts following each other onstage. For instance, an evening's entertainment might feature a singer followed by a tap dancer, then a trapeze artist, a magician, a banjo player, and a comedian. From 1880 to 1920, vaudeville acts played at theaters in big cities and small towns across the United States for a few days or several months at a time.

with laughter and applause. He later described how this incident inspired him to change his act:

> *Instead of trying to keep on with this single roping act I decided people wanted to see me catch something. So I went back home and marked me a place of ground about as big as a stage and started to work on the horse act.*

For the horse act, Rogers planned to use fancy throws to rope a man riding a horse across the stage. After years of perfecting his roping techniques, he produced spectacular throws for the audience. But making it work with a live horse on a tiny vaudeville stage required expert timing and awareness of the small space around him.

Throughout the fall of 1904, Rogers performed daily with the Mulhall Congress of Rough Riders and Ropers and practiced the horse act during his free time. It was enough to keep him quite busy, but something else soon grabbed his attention. Betty

Rogers simultaneously roped vaudeville star Buck McKee and his horse.

Blake, whom Rogers had not seen for more than four years, was visiting the Louisiana Purchase Exposition with one of her sisters. She heard about his cowboy act and decided to send him a note. He invited her to come see his show that day. But Betty was less than impressed when Rogers appeared onstage wearing the tight-fitting red velvet suit he had brought from Australia. She later said:

> *He looked so funny, and I was so embarrassed when my sister ... gave me sidelong glances and smiled at the costume, that I didn't hear the applause or find much joy in Will's expertness with the rope.*

Madison Square Garden, billed as "The World's Most Famous Arena," has been four different arenas. It first opened in 1879 as a cycling stadium at New York's Madison Square, at Madison Avenue and 23rd Street. In 1890, the cycling stadium was made into the stadium where Will Rogers appeared at the New York Horse Fair. This was New York City's second-tallest building at the time, and it featured seating for 8,000 guests, plus standing room for many more. In 1925, a new Madison Square Garden was built at 49th Street and Eighth Avenue. The current Madison Square Garden, on Seventh Avenue between 31st and 32nd streets, opened in 1968.

Still, Betty wrote Rogers a letter after seeing him, and soon they were corresponding regularly as he began traveling to more vaudeville engagements. Although Betty said she had not been too impressed by him, he certainly seemed impressed by her. From Chicago, he wrote:

> *I could just love a girl about your caliber, see. You know I was always kinder headstrong about you anyway. But I always thought that a cowboy dident come up to your Ideal.*

Will and Betty wrote to each other over the next year as he toured several Midwestern states.

In the spring of 1905, he took a job performing at the New York Horse Fair in New York City's Madison Square Garden. The show was managed by Zack Mulhall, the same man who had hired Rogers for the exposition a year earlier.

Although Rogers was not the star of the show, he soon got attention

The Mulhall Cowboy Carnival in Madison Square Garden

for his roping skills. One afternoon, one of the steers in the show jumped over the stage and ran up the stairs to a balcony packed with people. The *New York World* described what happened next: "Women screamed and men shouted" and the band "abandoned horns of all sizes and fled." Rogers ran after the steer, roped it, and ushered it back onto the stage. By the next day, after reading newspaper accounts of the event, many New Yorkers knew who Will Rogers was.

This new popularity helped him decide to stay in New York when Mulhall's show left a few months later. Rogers did not have a job, but he was determined to break into big-time vaudeville on the New York City stage. Then in June, after a month of practicing his act and trying to convince theater owners to hire him, he finally got a job at Keith's Union Square Theater. From there, his reputation quickly spread. Two days after appearing at Keith's, he was offered the chance to perform in two large U.S. cities—Boston and Philadelphia.

Soon Rogers had a long-term job at one of New York's most famous vaudeville theaters, and he was regularly touring throughout the United States and Europe. His first years of success may have been the result of a change he made in his act: He began speaking. Most vaudeville performances were silent, but Rogers often needed to describe a trick to the audience. One time, he made fun of himself for missing a trick, and the audience howled with laughter. Soon he prepared funny remarks for when he messed up. He even jotted down his favorite lines to use when he failed to rope his horse: "If I don't put one on soon [I] will have to give out rain checks," and "That's one thing I must say for that ferocious animal he was never much for sticking his neck into things."

Before long, Rogers was purposefully missing

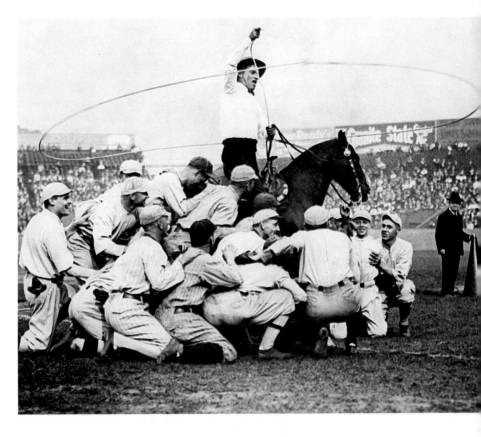

some of his throws to show how difficult the tricks were and to say things like, "Swinging a rope is all right, provided your neck ain't in it." Making fun of himself would become Rogers' trademark for the rest of his career. 🙰

Rogers displayed his roping talent, encircling an entire baseball team with his lariat.

6 Chapter

MARRIAGE AND SUCCESS

❧❧❧

As Will Rogers' stage career took off, he became more and more obsessed with another longtime goal: getting Betty Blake to marry him. He knew that having a successful career would help convince her to become his wife. He had written her a letter on the day he was offered the job at Keith's Union Square Theater, and for the next several years, the two kept in touch as Rogers traveled throughout the United States and Europe, performing three or four shows a day on the vaudeville circuit. He loved the friendships he developed with other vaudeville players—he even learned to ride a unicycle, juggle, and imitate voices—but he was determined to develop the one relationship he wanted most.

Rogers tried everything to get Betty Blake to

Will Rogers posed for a publicity photo early in his career.

marry him. He wrote long letters about how much she meant to him. He tried to make her jealous by telling her stories about other young women he met. But she turned down his marriage proposals in 1906 and 1907, telling him that they would always be friends, but she would not marry him. She did not want to be a vaudeville wife and have to travel all over the country.

Finally, in the fall of 1908, Rogers again asked Betty to marry him, and this time she said yes. She later said that he had told her he would soon end his vaudeville career and settle down in Oklahoma. Will and Betty were both 29 when they got married. The wedding was in Betty's hometown of Rogers, Arkansas, on November 25, 1908. Rogers later said:

> *When I roped her ... that was the star performance of my life.*

After the wedding, the couple went directly to New York City, where Betty got her first taste of show-business life. She was used to her small town in Arkansas, where everyone knew each other and went to the same dances and parties. In New York City, the Rogers lived in a hotel with actors and musicians. They ate in restaurants where the other diners were sometimes gamblers, wrestlers, and people considered unfit company in Betty's hometown. But

Will and Betty Rogers spent time in Atlantic City soon after their wedding.

Betty and Will spent only a few weeks in New York before heading out on the road.

The couple traveled throughout the country as Rogers performed in vaudeville. He was eager to introduce Betty to show-business life. As she later wrote:

> *His life had been full ... and he wanted me to know all about it—the bad along with the good—every little thing as far back as he could remember.*

Betty soon found that she liked the lifestyle. She wrote to friends and family that she enjoyed married life and had become "a pretty good cook." From Atlantic City, she wrote to Will's father, "We have had such a good time here that we sorter hate to leave."

The Rogerses' life changed in October 1911, when their son, William Vann Rogers, was born. The new father continued to travel the country performing, but Betty and the baby stayed in New York City.

The Rogers family had their first real apartment on New York's Upper West Side, and Rogers made an important career decision: After years of performing roping tricks onstage with a horse for a partner, it was time to launch a solo act. Audiences seemed to respond more to his humor than to his lariat skills. Plus, with a family to support, he could use the extra money he would save by not having to feed and house a horse.

To make up for the horse's absence, Rogers began adding new gimmicks to his acts. He started roping with one hand while doing something else with the other. He even threw ropes while riding a unicycle. He also began singing. Soon he was asked to appear in a musical show on Broadway, performing his act during a scenery change. His first Broadway appearance was in 1912, and over the next few years he was offered a few more opportunities to perform on Broadway.

As his career opportunities grew, so did the Rogers family. Mary Rogers was born in 1913 and

James in 1915. Now with a young family, Rogers was eager to spend more time at home.

In 1915, a talent scout for Florenz Ziegfeld, one of the country's biggest theater producers, asked him to appear in a daily show called the *Midnight Frolic*. This was a lavish variety show that took place at midnight

Rogers swung a lasso around himself and his three children.

Rogers' roping talent boosted his career and gave him exposure to various famous people.

in the rooftop nightclub of the New Amsterdam Theater. Rogers' salary was $175 per week—a little less than he earned on the vaudeville circuit, but now he gained more exposure to influential people. Each night, dozens of New York's swankiest residents attended the *Frolic* to sip cocktails, socialize, and be seen by other members of the city's elite social class.

Rogers' simple cowboy attitude was a big hit with the sophisticated New York crowd, but he soon learned he needed new material. Many people attended the *Frolic* night after night, so he could not use the same jokes that had amused his vaudeville audiences for years.

Betty suggested he use the daily news for his comedy. After all, everybody in the audience read the newspapers. So Rogers spent an hour each day combing through the papers for news that could be the topics of his jokes.

Rogers' humor about current events was so successful that he became a main attraction of the *Frolic*. Soon Ziegfeld asked him to star in the daily *Ziegfeld Foll-ies*. The *Follies* appeared in theaters throughout the United States and Canada. It was known for having beautiful dancers who appeared in stunning costumes. Between dance acts, comedians would fill the time so the dancers could get ready. This was supposed to be Rogers' role,

Florenz Ziegfeld (1867–1932)

Rogers (front center) took a curtain call after a Midnight Frolic *performance.*

but he was so popular that his name was soon being used to bring in customers.

Although Rogers spent much of the year away from his family, he earned a good income of $600 a week, more than enough to support his family of five. He also grew from being a New York celebrity to a national star during his first years appearing with the *Follies*.

Still known as a cowboy, Rogers continued to perform lariat throws, but more and more people attended the *Follies* for his comedy. They appreciated his simple humor. He made fun of himself and life's complications. He stated simple facts in a humorous way and pointed out how ridiculous current events sometimes were.

One of Rogers' favorite topics was the government. Although he became friends with politicians and appreciated what governments do for people, he understood that many people did not trust the government. Audiences related well to his humorous comments, such as this typical joke:

> *People often ask me, "Will, where do you get your jokes?" I just tell 'em, "Well, I watch the government and report the facts, that is all I do, and I don't even find it necessary to exaggerate."* 🦢

7 ON TO HOLLYWOOD

Chapter

꩜

By 1918, Will Rogers was enjoying being a star. With his success, he could spend more time with his family. Although he traveled part of the year with the *Follies*, he remained in New York where Betty was expecting their fourth child. Their son Fred was born July 15, 1918. Rogers taught all of his children to ride horses, and the family spent their days riding and playing near their New York home.

As always, Rogers was eager for new adventures. In those days, there was one form of entertainment that was considered more daring and adventurous than any other: silent movies. Rogers wanted to see if he could repeat his stage success on the screen, and in 1918, he got his chance. The movie *Laughing Bill Hyde* was filmed on the Goldwyn Pictures

Rogers and dancer Ann Pennington, a regular performer for the Follies

Corporation studio in New Jersey, just across the river from Manhattan where the *Follies* appeared nightly. For much of the summer, Rogers spent his days filming in New Jersey and his evenings performing in the *Follies*. The long days paid off; the film was a hit with both film critics and audiences. In November, Rogers signed a contract to star in movies for one year for Goldwyn Pictures.

In June 1919, he moved to Hollywood, California, the newly established movie capital of the world. He lived in temporary rooms for a few weeks until his family arrived. Since he was earning far more than he ever had before—$2,250 a week—he could afford to rent a huge house with a swimming pool in the Hancock Park section of Los Angeles. Rogers spent long days at the movie studios, but he had most evenings free to spend time with Betty and the children.

Betty wrote to Will's sister Maud about how much she enjoyed their first summer in Los Angeles:

> *We are very delighted with California. [We] have a nice house, very comfortable, such a beautiful yard, and the climate is perfectly wonderful—cool nights are really cold, and the air is glorious. ... It is quite a treat for us to have our evenings.*

Although there wasn't enough room for them

to ride horses in their yard, the movie studio built a stable in the studio lot, which was surrounded by plenty of open land for riding. Mary and Will Jr. rode their horses there almost every afternoon.

Rogers (right) was greeted by representatives from the Goldwyn Studio upon his arrival in Los Angeles.

Will Rogers made a dozen movies during the first two years he was in Hollywood. Although he came to be known as one of the country's greatest comedic actors, his earliest films were not comedies. Will's comedy relied on words, which wasn't suited to silent films. Instead, he starred in dramatic features during his early years in Hollywood.

One of the first was *Almost a Husband,* in which Rogers played Sam Lymna, a teacher in a small

Southern town. Sam is secretly in love with Eva, the town banker's daughter. At a house party one day, Sam plays a game in which he is supposed to act out the part of the groom in a mock wedding. The game rules state that the wedding will be performed by the next man who enters the party. But when the next man to enter the house turns out to be a real minister, the pretend vows become official and Sam and Eva are legally married. The movie's bad guy, Zeb Sawyer, is not pleased with this result, since he wants to marry Eva. For much of the movie, he tries to break up Sam and Eva, but in the end, Sam convinces Eva to honor the marriage. Will Rogers' good-guy character remains true to himself and wins the girl. This type of plot was repeated in several more of Rogers' films.

Unlike most silent film stars, he did not "overact" with his body and face. His acting style was similar to the way he told jokes to live audiences. At that time, though, the only way to add humor to a silent movie was in subtitles, or words written across the screen. The subtitles contained dialogue or funny comments about what was happening in the movie. The writers and directors at the studio soon realized that Will Rogers had the perfect dry sense of humor needed to create subtitles that American audiences would find funny. A newspaper reporter remembered seeing a man following Rogers around the studio with a clipboard and recalled, "The [studio] had engaged

him to do nothing else than trot around behind Rogers, the walking subtitle factory, to catch ... gems of repartee."

Rogers donned a cowboy outfit for one of his movie roles.

Most of Rogers' movies showcased his roping talents. Many had very similar plots, and Rogers usually played a good guy who was not particularly smart, confident, or attractive but managed to achieve success by accident. In *Jubilo*, the most successful film he made for Goldwyn, Rogers played a tramp who was almost framed for a train robbery. Although the tramp is lazy and unsuccessful in life, he is a good guy underneath, and through honesty and courage he ends up leading the police to the real villain. Rogers summed up the plot himself:

> *Story? ... Same as usual. Looks bad for the hero right up to the last Close Up. First reel introduces Hero dividing last crum [crumb] of bread with dog. ... Second reel looks bad for hero. Third reel looks even worse for hero. Fourth reel all evidence points to hero being the robber. Villain looks slick and satisfied. End reel five the winners. The tramp wins 100 percent HERO.*

Jubilo was named after a popular short story, as well as its theme song, a well-known spiritual called "In the Days of Jubilo." Rogers was savvy enough to know that this name would stick with moviegoers, but at one point the director wanted to change the movie's title to a longer phrase. Usually, directors would make their own decisions about titles and not consult their actors. But when Rogers heard

Rogers played with a lasso while he took notes for one of his movies.

about the possible name change, he sent a telegram to the director: "Thought I was supposed to be the comedian but when you suggest changing the title of Jubilo you are funnier than I ever was." To prove his point about how perfect the short-and-sweet title of *Jubilo* was, Rogers included about 10 tongue-in-cheek suggestions for new titles, including *A Spotted Horse but He Is Only Painted*, *The Vagabond with a Heart as Big as His Appetite*, *He Loses in the First Reel but Wins in the Last*, and *The Old Man Left but the Tramp Protected Her*. In the end, the director

The 1920s was a decade of much change in the United States. New technology popularized many items including the telephone, the radio, and the affordable car. It was also a period of great social change. More American women began demanding equal treatment, such as voting rights and equal pay. Widespread wealth made leisure time and activities available to more Americans than ever before. But the rapid pace of change made many Americans uncomfortable, as seen in the Prohibition law of 1920, which outlawed alcoholic beverages. To those who felt uneasy or confused by the Roaring Twenties, Will Rogers provided a dose of simple, honest values.

took Rogers' advice and kept the name *Jubilo*—and the movie was a hit.

Rogers made fun of the simple plots of his movies, but he did not mind them at all. He liked the fact that the films emphasized his country upbringing and reflected good moral values. He wanted entire families to be able to watch his movies. In fact, Will Rogers became known as one of Hollywood's "cleanest" stars, at a time when the movie capital was known for the wild behavior of many of its stars.

The Rogers family enjoyed the California lifestyle. They spent much of their time outside, riding and playing other sports. By the end of 1919, they had moved to Beverly Hills. In 1920, Rogers renewed his contract with the studio for one more year at $3,000 a week. Just weeks before he signed the contract extension, his youngest son, Fred, died unexpectedly from diphtheria. Rogers' other sons later said that their father was devastated by

Rogers' Beverly Hills home included a large riding ring.

Fred's death, but that he never once talked about it.

Instead, Rogers threw himself into his career. When his contract with Goldwyn ended, he decided to produce his own movies. This way, he would have a say in everything about the movies, from writing the scripts and choosing the director to acting the lead roles.

Rogers soon found out that making movies was expensive. After spending almost $50,000 of his own money to make three films, the company that was supposed to distribute them said it would need five more films before it released any of them. He was unwilling to take the chance of losing any more money, so he shut down Will Rogers Productions after one year. It was the first failure that he had experienced in more than 15 years of a successful career.

In The Ropin' Fool, the first movie produced by Will Rogers Productions, Rogers played "Ropes" Reilly, a man who spent his days and nights roping anything that moved. The film, which was released two years after it was filmed, was a perfect showcase for his remarkable lariat-throwing skills.

Rogers needed to make up the money he had lost, so he left his family in California and returned to New York and the vaudeville stage. He performed in some of the same theaters he had performed in several years earlier, but now he was making 10 times as much money. His first engagement was for $3,000 a week. Soon he signed up to headline the *Midnight Frolic* at the New Amsterdam Theater again. By 1922, he was also starring in the *Follies* in New York again.

Rogers also branched out into a new form of entertainment: public speaking. Businesses and other large gatherings were always looking for speakers to highlight dinner engagements, and Rogers soon became one of the most sought-after speakers on the dinner circuit. Many evenings, he would give a speech at a dinner and then rush over to

the New Amsterdam to perform in the *Follies* or the
Midnight Frolic.

Back in Hollywood, two of the three Will Rogers
Production films were finally released. Between his
salary from the *Follies*, his speaking engagements,
and his share of the film profits, Rogers was able to
repay his large debts. ☙

A director shouted instructions during the filming of Doubling for Romeo *as Will and his son Jim looked on.*

8 WRITING AND OTHER VENTURES

✦

It took Will Rogers only a few years to recover his losses from his movie-producing experiment in the early 1920s. For the rest of the decade, he continued to prove his popularity as a film star, but he also found new areas of entertainment.

Rogers had first journeyed into the world of writing in 1916 when he sent articles to various newspapers. Three years later, he wrote a book of humorous passages—each about one paragraph long—about the peace conference that was being held in Europe after the end of World War I. The book, called *Rogers-isms: The Cowboy Philosopher on the Peace Conference*, had been successful, but Rogers had become too busy with film work to return to writing.

> *Hollywood of the 1920s was known for the wild lives of its celebrities. Will Rogers was friends with several movie stars, but he often wrote about his disapproval of the "Hollywood lifestyle." To not offend anyone, his comments were always laced with humor, such as "Hollywood may not keep you young, but it sure keeps you marrying."*

By 1922, he was living in New York again, and he took up writing in a different form. He began a weekly newspaper column that was bought and published by newspapers all over the country, including *The New York Times*. The columns were up to 1,500 words, and he wrote about a wide variety of current events. He used the same tone and language that he used onstage, which meant that he often used questionable grammar and spelling, such as his frequent use of the word *ain't*.

His topics ranged from politics to families to celebrities, many of whom he knew personally and was able to make fun of in a good-natured way. Like all of his humor, Rogers' writing made people feel good. He reminded them that certain aspects of modern life confused everyone. For instance, Rogers did not like how banks loaned people money in the form of mortgages on their properties. Since the bank can take the property if the mortgage loan cannot be repaid, Rogers said:

> *Borrowing money on what's called "easy terms," is a one-way ticket to the Poor*

Rogers made time for his children despite a busy schedule.

House. Show me ten men that mortgage this land to get money and I will have to get a search warrant to find one that gets the land back again. If you think it ain't a Sucker Game, why is your Banker the richest man in your Town? Why is your Bank the biggest and finest building in your Town?

Rogers displayed one of his trademark styles in the same banking column. He often related a current problem facing the country to his own upbringing in the Oklahoma plains. He reminded people that the simple values he was raised with could help people avoid much of life's difficulties. He wrote:

> *I was raised on a Cattle Ranch and I never saw or heard of a Ranchman going broke. Only the ones who had borrowed money. You can't break a man that don't borrow; he may not have anything, but Boy! he can look the World in the face and say, "I don't owe ... a nickel."*

Although Rogers was becoming one of the richest men in the country, he showed people he understood their worries and concerns. He made fun of himself and reminded people he did not consider himself to be one of the bigwigs he worked and socialized with. He showed this attitude when he continued in his column about banks:

> *You will say, what will all the Bankers do [if they can't make money from mortgages]? I don't care what they do. Let 'em go to work, if there is a job any of them could earn a living at. Banking and After Dinner Speaking are two of the most Nonessential industries we have in this country. I am ready to reform if they are.*

Although Rogers was quick to make fun of

himself, he only made fun of others if he thought they could take his joking. He once said: "I don't think I ever hurt any man's feelings by my little gags. I know I never willfully did it. When I have to do that to make a living, I will quit."

Rogers' newspaper writing made him more popular around the United States and the world.

Although he did not view himself as a bigwig, Will Rogers (left) posed with Henry Ford, the founder of the Ford Motor Company, and an actor dressed as Abraham Lincoln.

Suddenly, hundreds of thousands of people were reading his weekly columns. Anticipation of what his next column would cover became a topic of conversation from coast to coast. Guessing that Rogers' fans would jump at the chance to see him in person, a concert promoter paid him to do a five-month tour across the country. Rogers was booked

Rogers spent much of his time polishing the material for his column.

nightly in concert halls, town halls, and school gyms in more than 20 states. The tour was a huge success, and Rogers repeated it several times throughout the 1920s.

In 1926, the editor of one of the most popular magazines in the country, *The Saturday Evening Post*, offered Rogers a job as a reporter from Europe. His weekly articles would be about life in Europe and sent to U.S. President Calvin Coolidge. Rogers took his family to Europe with him and sent home weekly "reports" to the magazine featuring his down-to-earth views on European life. These articles were immensely popular with American readers.

Also in 1926, Rogers began writing a short daily column called "Will Rogers Says" that was syndicated, or sold to hundreds of newspapers. At about 100 to 200 words, it usually focused on an event that had taken place the previous day. Like the weekly column, it contained his simple grammar and style. The editor of *The New York Times* wrote to his staff about Rogers' style:

> *Please do not correct Will Rogers' English or spelling. His little pieces are unique because he makes his own English. When you "improve" it you are taking away part of the personality he is selling to readers.*

9 AIRWAYS AND AIRWAVES

∽⌒⌒∽

By the end of the 1920s, Will Rogers was one of America's biggest stars. He had conquered stage, film, and newspapers. In 1929, he found yet another way to connect with the American public: by acting in his first talking film, a technology that was still brand new. Over the next six years, he starred in 21 talking movies and became an even bigger star than he had been in silent movies. His unique style of humor was much more effective when he could voice his thoughts without subtitles.

Meanwhile, other new technology was providing more ways of connecting people. Rogers was fascinated with inventions, such as the airplane. He had first flown in 1915, when he had paid $5 for a ride in a "flying boat" that took off from the ocean by

Rogers timidly took the hand of actress Fifi D'Orsay in 1929 during his first talking film, They Had to See Paris.

Atlantic City, New Jersey. In the mid-1920s, Rogers had become more and more interested in flying, and he sometimes flew between engagements around the country.

Wiley Post removed the eye patch from his left eye for a photograph.

He met one famous flyer, Wiley Post, when Post flew Rogers to a rodeo in Oklahoma in 1925. Post was known for being a daredevil pilot, and many people were turned off by his gruff manner and rough appearance—he wore an eye patch for most of his life after losing an eye as a teenager. But Rogers admired Post's immense flying skills—and risk-taking nature—and the two began a long friendship.

Rogers also became friends with another famous pilot of the day, Charles Lindbergh. Unlike Post, Lindbergh was known for his quiet, modest behavior. He had charmed and amazed the world with his solo air flight across the Atlantic Ocean in May 1927. At the time, Rogers showed his own awe over the effort, putting aside his usual joking style in his writing:

No attempt at jokes today. A slim, tall, bashful, smiling American boy is somewhere out over the middle of the Atlantic Ocean, where no lone human being has ever ventured before. He is being prayed for to every kind of Supreme Being that has a following. If he is lost it will be the most universally regretted single loss we ever had. But that kid ain't going to fail.

Charles Lindbergh (left) and Will Rogers shared an interest in aviation.

Four months later, Rogers was invited to speak at a banquet in San Diego honoring Lindbergh. He enthusiastically accepted the invitation, and the next day, he received an even more exciting offer.

Lindbergh asked if Will and Betty Rogers would like to fly from San Diego to Los Angeles with him. They happily agreed to come along. While Lindbergh was in the cockpit, he noticed that the plane was becoming tail heavy. When he came out of the cockpit, he found the problem: Ten of the 11 passengers were crowded around Will and Betty, while the remaining passenger took their photograph.

Despite this problem, the flight went smoothly, and less than a month later, Rogers took his own coast-to-coast flight. There were no passenger flights in those days, but he was allowed to fly on a U.S. mail flight—paying $814 for his weight in postage stamps. From that day on, Rogers was a strong supporter of air travel. He was convinced that it would be the wave of the future.

He also liked the similarities between the pioneer days of air travel and the Wild West of his youth. He once said that pilots reminded him of cowboys. He became friends with many of the era's most famous pilots. His friend Wiley Post would set a speed record in 1933 by flying solo around the world in seven days, 18 hours, and 49 minutes.

Rogers worked hard to promote air travel in the United States and to show the public how safe it was. He was so concerned with publicizing air safety that when he once broke all of his ribs in an emergency landing, he stayed away from public appearances

Rogers eagerly promoted air travel to the public.

and kept the news out of the papers so it would not alarm potential air travelers.

Soon he was flying all over the world, visiting London, Manchuria, Java, Egypt, South America, Japan, and Moscow. He often visited countries as a reporter, sending back daily and weekly columns of his observations. He also used air travel as a way to quickly connect with people in need. For much of his career, Rogers had tried to use his fame to help others. For instance, in 1927, he ended his spring speaking tour of the United States with a benefit performance in New Orleans for victims of a huge flood that killed 214 people and left thousands homeless. In 1931, he used air travel to perform in 50 towns over a span of 18 days that benefited victims of a devastating drought in Oklahoma, Arkansas, and Texas. That same year, he traveled to Nicaragua to benefit victims of earthquakes and fires.

At the end of the 1920s, the Rogers family moved a few miles west from their Beverly Hills home to a secluded hilltop ranch in Pacific Palisades. Rogers had bought the property in 1924, attracted by the rugged undeveloped hillside that reminded him of wide-open Oklahoma. But the hills were steep, and there were no paved roads to access the property. Rogers oversaw the construction

During the Roaring Twenties, millions of Americans increased their wealth by investing in fast-rising stocks and using mortgage loans to buy property. But in October 1929, the stock market crashed—leaving people across America with worthless stocks and no way to pay their bank loans. Banks began to close and many people lost their life savings, leading to the Great Depression of the 1930s. Although most Americans were affected by the nationwide lack of money, jobs, and even food, those who had not invested in stocks or taken out large mortgage loans were better off than most.

of a road that climbed up the 200 feet (61 m) from Beverly Boulevard, using four switchbacks to tackle the steep hill. The whole Rogers family helped plant dozens of small eucalyptus trees to help stabilize the hillside earth.

Rogers first built a barn to keep his horses on the land. Soon after, he built a summerhouse, but he insisted that it be Oklahoma-style rather than Beverly Hills-style. When the family sold the Beverly Hills house and moved to the ranch full-time, they added a two-story, 13-room house to the weekend "box house" they had already built. But even this

Jim (from left), Bill, Mary, Will, and Betty Rogers

By the time the Rogers family moved to the Pacific Palisades ranch home, Will Rogers was such an avid polo player that he included polo grounds on the property. Polo consists of two teams of horseback-riding players using long-handled mallets to score balls in the opposite team's goal. Polo was a favorite pastime of other Hollywood celebrities as well during that time.

new house was kept simple. When an architect submitted plans for an Italian-Spanish villa with a marble fireplace, Will threw them out and asked for a copy of the blueprints for a Montana ranch house he had recently visited.

While they partly moved to Pacific Palisades to gain some privacy, Rogers really craved a Western-style ranch home. He admitted that the property was "not really a ranch, but we call it that. It sounds big and don't really do no harm." His children had ridden horses since they were toddlers, and the ranch featured stables, a riding ring, and polo grounds for the family to use. Both with and without his children, Rogers began to spend hours in the riding ring, practicing his roping skills. He practiced the same tricks as when he was a teenager, except now he roped calves instead of steers.

Rogers found another passion in the early 1930s: airwaves. Radio was beginning to become the biggest form of mass communication at the time. With its ability to reach large portions of the country, radio provided an ideal platform for Rogers' art. In 1930, he signed up to do 12 15-minute talks for radio. Radio producers were so eager to have him that he was paid $77,000, the same amount the famous baseball player Babe Ruth was paid for the entire year.

In 1932, Rogers became a regular on a radio version of the *Ziegfeld Follies*. But with only four minutes per show allotted to him, Rogers found it difficult to connect with the audience, and his role was soon cut. A year later, he was offered his own half-hour live show on Sunday evenings. The

President Franklin Delano Roosevelt (left) threw his head back to laugh during Will Rogers' (far right) broadcast.

show was called *The Good Gulf Show*, which was sponsored by the Gulf Oil Company. The show was another success, with millions of listeners across the United States tuning in.

Although radio can be challenging to comedians—they cannot see their audience's reactions to know if the jokes are going over well—Rogers found that his off-the-cuff style was perfect on the air. Listeners liked the fact that he often made up his script as he went along, unlike most other radio performers of the day, who were tightly scripted.

Rogers wore a mix of medieval armor and cowboy apparel for the 1931 movie A Connecticut Yankee.

By the mid-1930s, there was no doubt that Will Rogers was America's most popular personality. His huge success on the radio increased his fans, but his enormous fame in movies and newspapers continued as well. The Sunday radio show was the most popular weekly show in the country, and between his daily and weekly columns, he was the most read columnist in the country. In 1933, he was also the country's second-biggest Hollywood star (after Marie Dressler) and its most popular male star. In 1934, he was the largest box-office draw.

Rogers continued his round-the-clock work, but he also took time to enjoy his family and his favorite pastime: flying. In 1934, he took a two-month around-the-world trip with Betty and their sons, Jim and Bill. They flew first to Hawaii, where they had dinner with President Franklin Delano Roosevelt and his wife, Eleanor. Then it was on to Japan and Russia, where they got stuck for six days on a train waiting for an airplane to arrive to fly them to Moscow. From Moscow, Bill and Jim flew home to California for college, while Will and Betty continued on through Europe. This would be the couple's last trip together. ✍

10 A Tragic End

◦⟨✕⟩◦

It was a cold, foggy day in the northern part of Alaska, and Will Rogers was completing one of the biggest adventures of his life. He and his pilot friend, Wiley Post, had been traveling throughout Alaska for more than a week. They were on a mission to survey a route through Alaska for flying mail and passenger planes between Russia and the United States.

For this mission, Post had spent weeks piecing together an airplane made out of various other plane parts. As he worked on his plane in a huge warehouse in Burbank, California, Rogers—who was not part of the trip at that point—often visited him. The two would talk about flying, and Rogers even learned a little about the mechanics of airplanes. Post was so excited to get going on his adventure that he may

Rogers bundled up in warm clothing in preparation for his trip to Alaska.

have taken some shortcuts in assembling his plane. Because he would be flying over so much water in Alaska, he knew he wanted to add floats to the regular landing gear. When the floats he had ordered were delayed, he decided to make do with others he found. But these floats were for a much larger plane, and adding them increased the chance that his plane would become nose-heavy and possibly crash during takeoff.

When Post's flying partner for the Alaska trip canceled at the last minute, he asked the 55-year old Rogers to go with him. Rogers talked to Betty and thought about it for a few days, but he knew he could not turn down this chance for adventure. The two men set out in early August 1935. As Rogers wrote in one of his weekly columns:

> Was you ever driving around in a car and not knowing or caring where you went? ... Well, that's what Wiley and I are doing. We sure are having a great time. If we hear of whales or polar bears in the Arctic, or a big herd of caribou, we fly over and see it.

But on this day, Rogers and Post were on a more specific adventure. They were determined to land at Point Barrow, the northernmost piece of land in North America. Point Barrow was not on the way to

the pair's next destination, and reaching it required a dangerous 500-mile (800-km) journey over the Endicott Mountains. But Rogers insisted on the side trip; he knew the adventure would make a great topic for a newspaper column. Before leaving, he sent a telegram to his daughter, Mary, who was beginning her own acting career. That week, she was acting in a play about a girl whose father dies in a plane crash. Rogers sent her a telegram that read:

Rogers (left) and Post (second from right) prepared to leave for Point Barrow, Alaska.

Great trip. Wish you were along. How's your acting? ... Going to Point Barrow today. Furthest point of land north on whole American continent. Don't worry. Dad.

Rogers and Post were so eager to leave that they took off before they received the day's weather report. If they had waited, they would have learned that visibility was "zero-zero" because of dense fog. Unable to see, Post landed the small plane in a lagoon and Rogers got out to ask some Inuit the way to Point Barrow. The two men climbed back in their plane and took off.

A group of Inuit witnessed the plane wreck from a distance.

Minutes later, the plane nose-dived into the lagoon, and the impact killed both men instantly. The

Inuit who had given them directions called to the men but got no response. Realizing that they were dead, the man ran for five hours to alert authorities at an Army base about the crash. When he reported the victims to the sergeant on duty as one with a patch on his eye and the other as a large man wearing boots, the sergeant realized he was talking about Wiley Post and Will Rogers.

It took another day for news of Will Rogers' death to reach the American public. People were stunned. Across the country, newspaper and radio headlines carried the tragic news. Thousands of fans poured into the Hollywood Bowl arena for a memorial service. Across the United States, people who had enjoyed Will Rogers' sense humor mourned.

Rogers was originally buried in California, but in 1944, his body was moved—along with his son Fred's body—to the Will Rogers Memorial Museum in Claremore, Oklahoma. When Betty died later in 1944, she was buried next to Will and Fred.

Lasting tributes to Will Rogers are found throughout the United States. Will Rogers State Historic Park offers public tours of his

> *Rogers State University in Oklahoma was named after Will Rogers. Statues of Will Rogers on his horse stand in three spots: the Will Rogers Memorial Center in Fort Worth, Texas; the campus of Texas Tech University; and the Will Rogers Memorial Museum in Claremore. The rear end of the Texas Tech horse faces Texas A&M University, a football rival of the school.*

Pacific Palisades ranch house, stable, riding fields, and polo grounds. The Oklahoma house he was born in is also open to the public. In California, the famous Route 66 is known as Will Rogers Highway, and Oklahoma has the Will Rogers Turnpike. A U.S. Navy submarine, as well as the airport in Oklahoma City, Oklahoma, were named after the famous entertainer.

The City of Beverly Hills honored Will Rogers by establishing a memorial park in his name.

Rogers was honored with two stars on Hollywood's legendary Hollywood Walk of Fame—one for radio and one for film. He is also remembered at Disney's Epcot Center, where a robotic Will Rogers

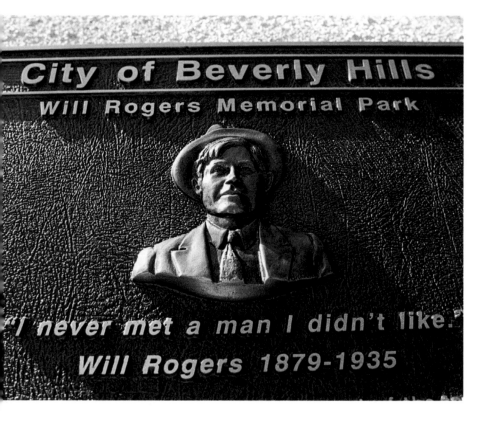

City of Beverly Hills
Will Rogers Memorial Park

"I never met a man I didn't like."
Will Rogers 1879-1935

twirls his lariat. In 1991, actor Keith Carradine played Rogers on Broadway in the Tony Award–winning musical, *The Will Rogers Follies: A Life in Revue.*

Will Rogers' caring and humorous personality will always be remembered. Five years before his death, he wrote:

> *When I die, my epitaph or whatever you call those signs on gravestones is going to read: 'I joked about every prominent man of my time, but I never met a man I dident like.' I am so proud of that I can hardly wait to die so it can be carved. And when you come to my grave you will find me sitting there proudly reading it.*

ROGERS' LIFE

1879

Born November 4 in Indian Territory, near present-day Oologah, Oklahoma

1890

Mother dies

1898

Drops out of Kemper School and takes a job as a ranch hand in Texas

1895

1879

Thomas Edison invents electric lights

1883

Brooklyn Bridge opens to traffic after 14 years of construction

1896

The first modern Olympic Games are held in Athens, Greece

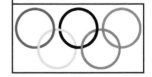

WORLD EVENTS

1904
Completes his round-the-world trip, sailing home from New Zealand

1905
Appears with the New York Horse Fair in Madison Square Garden

1908
Marries Betty Blake; the two return to New York together

1905

1904
Cy Young of the Boston Americans pitches the first perfect game in modern baseball history

1903
Brothers Orville and Wilbur Wright successfully fly a powered airplane

1909
Explorers Robert E. Peary and Matthew Henson and four Inuit reach the North Pole; they mark the spot with an American flag

ROGERS' LIFE

1912

Appears in a Broadway show for the first time, providing comic relief and rope twirling between scenes

1911

Son Will Rogers Jr. is born; father dies

1913

Daughter Mary is born

1910

1914

Archduke Francis Ferdinand is assassinated, launching World War I (1914–1918)

1911

Fire at the Triangle Shirtwaist Factory in New York City kills 145 people, mostly girls

1912

The *Titanic* sinks on its maiden voyage; more than 1,500 people die

1913

Henry Ford begins to use standard assembly lines to produce automobiles

WORLD EVENTS

1915

Appears in Ziegfeld's *Midnight Frolic* at New York's New Amsterdam Theater; son Jim is born

1918

Son Fred is born; acts in his first silent film

1919

Moves to California with family; begins silent film work for Goldwyn Studios; publishes his first book of humorous passages

1915

1916

German-born physicist Albert Einstein publishes his general theory of relativity

1919

The Treaty of Versailles officially ends World War I

1920

American women get the right to vote

ROGERS' LIFE

1922

Returns to work on the New York stage; begins a weekly newspaper column, which he would write for the rest of his life

1926

Tours Europe on assignment for *The Saturday Evening Post*; begins writing a daily syndicated newspaper column

1929

Stars in his first talking film

1925

1923

French actress Sarah Bernhardt dies

1928

Walt Disney makes the first sound cartoon, *Steamboat Willy* starring Mickey Mouse

1929

The U.S. stock market crashes, and severe worldwide economic depression sets in

WORLD EVENTS

1934

Ranked Hollywood's number-one box-office attraction

1933

Stars in his own weekly half-hour live radio show on Sunday evenings

1935

Dies August 1 in a plane crash near Point Barrow, Alaska

1935

1933

Nazi leader Adolf Hitler is named chancellor of Germany

1934

The Dionne quintuplets, the world's first quints to survive, are born in Canada

1932

The infant son of Anne Morrow Lindbergh and Charles Lindbergh is kidnapped and murdered

DATE OF BIRTH: November 4, 1879

BIRTHPLACE: Indian Territory, near present-day Oologah, Oklahoma

FATHER: Clement Vann Rogers (1839–1911)

MOTHER: Mary America Schrimsher (1839–1890)

EDUCATION: Through 10th grade

SPOUSE: Betty Blake (1879–1944)

DATE OF MARRIAGE: November 25, 1908

CHILDREN: William Rogers Jr. (1911–1993)
Mary Rogers (1913–1989)
James (Jimmy) Rogers (1915–2000)
Fred Stone Rogers (1918–1920)

DATE OF DEATH: August 15, 1935

PLACE OF BURIAL: Claremore, Oklahoma

FURTHER READING

Alter, Judy. *Vaudeville: The Birth of Show Business*. London: Franklin Watts, 1998.

Bennett, Cathereen. *Will Rogers: Quotable Cowboy*. Minneapolis: Runestone Press, 1995.

Callan, Jim. *America in the 1930s*. New York: Facts on File, 2005.

Malone, Mary. *Will Rogers: Cowboy Philosopher*. Berkeley Heights, N.J.: Enslow Publishers, 1996.

LOOK FOR MORE SIGNATURE LIVES
BOOKS ABOUT THIS ERA:

Clara Barton: *Founder of the American Red Cross*

George Washington Carver: *Scientist, Inventor, and Teacher*

Amelia Earhart: *Legendary Aviator*

Thomas Alva Edison: *Great American Inventor*

Yo-Yo Ma: *Internationally Acclaimed Cellist*

Thurgood Marshall: *Civil Rights Lawyer and Supreme Court Justice*

Annie Oakley: *American Sharpshooter*

Amy Tan: *Writer and Storyteller*

Madame C.J. Walker: *Entrepreneur and Millionaire*

Booker T. Washington: *Innovative Educator*

On the Web

For more information on this topic,
use FactHound.

1. Go to *www.facthound.com*
2. Type in this book ID: 0756524636
3. Click on the *Fetch It* button.

FactHound will find the best
Web sites for you.

Historic Sites

Will Rogers State Historic Park
1501 Will Rogers State Park Road
Pacific Palisades, CA 90272
310/454-8212
Rogers' home in Pacific Palisades

Will Rogers Memorial Museum
1720 W. Will Rogers Blvd.
Claremore, OK 74017
800/324-9455
Museum with the world's largest collection
of artifacts and papers from Will Rogers,
as well as the Rogerses' family tomb

diphtheria
serious infection of the throat

drought
long period of extremely dry weather when there
is not enough rain to grow crops

gauchos
South American cowboys

subtitles
written words added to silent movies that contain
dialogue or explain the plot

syndicated
to sell an article or comic strip to multiple
magazines or newspapers to be published
at the same time

vaudeville
type of variety theater popular in the late 19th
and early 20th centuries that consisted of singing,
dancing, and comedy acts

Source Notes

Chapter 1

Page 11, line 13: "The Official Site of Will Rogers." CMG Worldwide.
9 Nov. 2006. www.cmgworldwide.com/historic/rogers/quotes5.htm

Chapter 2

Page 16, line 25: Ben Yagoda. *Will Rogers: A Biography*. New York: Knopf,
1993, p. 12.

Page 19, sidebar: Martin, Ken. "History of the Cherokee." cherokeehistory.com.
9 Nov. 2006. http://cherokeehistory.com/

Page 19, line 18: Ibid., p. 16.

Chapter 3

Page 23, line 9: Ibid., p. 18.

Page 23, line 27: Ibid., p. 22.

Page 24, line 7: Ibid.

Page 26, line 4: Ibid., p. 25.

Chapter 4

Page 31, line 16: "Will Rogers Memorial Museums in Claremore, Oklahoma."
Will Rogers Memorial Museums. 28 Aug. 2006. www.willrogers.com/
index3.html

Page 32, line 21: *Will Rogers: A Biography*, p. 43.

Page 34, line 15: Ibid., p. 56.

Page 34, line 23: Ibid., p. 62.

Page 35, line 3: Ibid., p. 64.

Chapter 5

Page 37, line 7: Ibid., p. 67.

Page 38, line 13: Ibid., p. 72.

Page 40, line 4: Ibid., pp. 74–75.

Page 41, line 9: Ibid., pp. 75–76.

Page 42, line 9: Ibid., p. 77.

Page 43, line 4: Ibid., p. 85.

Page 44, line 23: Ibid., p. 94.

Page 45, line 2: Bryan B. Sterling and Frances N. Sterling. *Will Rogers' World:
America's Foremost Political Humorist Comments on the Twenties and
Thirties—and Eighties and Nineties*. New York: M. Evans and Co., 1989, p. 4.

Chapter 6

Page 48, line 16: Ibid.

Page 49, line 7: *Will Rogers: A Biography*, p. 119.

Page 50, line 1: Ibid., p. 120.

Page 55, line 17: *Will Rogers' World: America's Foremost Political Humorist Comments on the Twenties and Thirties—and Eighties and Nineties*, p. 91.

Chapter 7

Page 58, line 21: *Will Rogers: A Biography*, p. 171.

Page 60, line 28: Ibid., p. 166.

Page 62, line 12: Ibid., p. 167.

Page 63, line 2: Ibid., p. 168.

Chapter 8

Page 70, sidebar: *Will Rogers' World: America's Foremost Political Humorist Comments on the Twenties and Thirties—and Eighties and Nineties*, p. 40.

Page 70, line 26: Ibid., p. 198.

Page 72, line 5: Ibid.

Page 72, line 20: Ibid.

Page 73, line 2: Ibid., p. 218.

Page 75, line 22: *Will Rogers: A Biography*, p. 249.

Chapter 9

Page 79, line 1: Ibid., p. 250.

Page 84, line 12: Ibid., p. 265.

Chapter 10

Page 90, line 17: Ibid., p. 327.

Page 92, line 1: Ibid., p. 328.

Page 95, line 8: "Respectfully Quoted: A Dictionary of Quotations Requested from the Congressional Research Service." Bartleby.com. Aug. 2003. 1 Nov. 2006. www.bartleby.com/73/

Collins, Reba, ed. *Will Rogers Says*. Tulsa, Okla.: Council Oak Books, 1992.

Martin, Ken. "History of the Cherokee." 2001. 28 Aug. 2006. http://cherokeehistory.com/

"The Official Site of Will Rogers." CMG Worldwide. 10 Aug. 2006. www.cmgworldwide.com/historic/rogers/biography.htm

"Respectfully Quoted: A Dictionary of Quotations Requested from the Congressional Research Service." Bartleby.com. Aug. 2003. 1 Nov. 2006. www.bartleby.com/73/

Sterling, Bryan B., and Frances N. Sterling. *Will Rogers' World: America's Foremost Political Humorist Comments on the Twenties and Thirties—and Eighties and Nineties*. New York: M. Evans and Co., 1989.

"Will Rogers Home Page." Southwestern Bell. 28 Aug. 2006. www.willrogers.org/

"Will Rogers Memorial Museums in Claremore, Oklahoma." Will Rogers Memorial Museums. 28 Aug. 2006. www.willrogers.com/index3.html

Yagoda, Ben. *Will Rogers: A Biography*. New York: Knopf, 1993.

Sandy Donovan has written several books for young readers about history, economics, government, and other topics. She has also worked as a newspaper reporter, a magazine editor, and a Web site developer. She has a bachelor's degree in journalism and a master's degree in public policy, and lives in Minneapolis, Minnesota, with her husband and two sons.

Image Credits